Gus & Jo: The Early Years

A Prequel Story from the Where the Pines Still Stand Universe

Kelly Schweiger

First Edition

Dedication

For those who endure.
For those who build anyway.
For those who refuse to give up.

READING ORDER

For the best experience, read in the following order:

THE CALLAHAN SERIES

1. Last Light
2. Winter's Bite
3. Enduring Fight

CHILDREN OF THE PINES

1. What Remains
2. What Divides
3. What Endures

EARLY YEARS Novellas

These can be read at any time after Book 1:

Gus & Jo

The First Stranger

Becoming Us

COMPANION STORIES

Callahan Family Pantry

A Light in the Dark

The Walkabout

Welcome to the world of the Callahans.

When the lights go out, survival isn't just about food and shelter—

it's about family, resilience, and the choices that define who we become.

If you enjoy post-apocalyptic survival, strong family bonds,

and character-driven stories of endurance and hope…

You're in the right place.

Contents

CHAPTER 1

Before

Morning came slow and gray, seeping through the thin curtains like it had somewhere better to be but couldn't quite manage the effort.

Jo knew the feeling. She was already awake, lying still, listening.

The tiny house had its own language — wood settling, a faint draft near the window, the quiet shift of someone moving in the next room. Not true silence. Just the absence of voices.

For now.

Beside her, Gus slept on his side, one arm thrown across the space between them like he'd reached for her in the night and stopped halfway. His breathing was steady. Unbothered.

Jo watched him for a moment.

Then she closed the gap, settling under his arm where she fit.

His hand tightened instinctively.

"You're awake," he muttered sleepily.

"I was trying not to be."

"Bad plan, work to do."

She huffed softly.

"Usually is."

The floor was cold.

Jo crossed the room in quick, quiet steps, pulling a sweater over her head as she went. The house was very small — two rooms and a narrow kitchen — but it held heat well enough if they kept the fire fed.

She stirred the coals now, coaxing them back to life, adding a piece of wood and watching for the flame to catch.

Outside, something moved across the yard.

Not an animal.

Jo glanced toward the window and relaxed.

Marcus, already up and moving.

Of course he was. That boy never seemed to sleep.

He came in a few minutes later without knocking, bringing the cold with him.

"Fence held," he said.

Jo nodded.

"That's good."

Marcus stepped out of his boots near the door and set them in line without thinking. Snow clung to the edges, already melting onto the boards.

"You been out long?" she asked.

"Couple hours."

She gave him a look.

"Don't you ever sleep. I thought teenagers slept all day."

He shrugged.

"Didn't feel like sleeping."

Gus came in a minute later, slower, still pulling on his coat as he walked.

"You checking my work out there?" he asked.

Marcus didn't look up.

"Just making sure it holds, brother."

Gus snorted.

"Bold of you to assume it wouldn't."

Marcus's mouth shifted slightly.

"Just verifying."

Jo turned away to hide the small smile that came with it.

The door swung open before the room could settle.

"Jesus, Mary, and Joseph, do any of you sleep?"

Liam Callahan filled the doorway with his voice before the rest of him arrived. Cold air followed him in, sharp and immediate.

Maeve stepped in behind, closing the door with a firm push.

"They're up, aren't they, Liam?" she said. "What more do you want?"

"I want them up earlier," Liam answered. "There are things to do, woman."

"You want a lot of things."

"And I don't get half of them."

"That's because you're unreasonable."

Gus leaned against the counter, watching them with the patience of a man who'd witnessed this exact conversation in a hundred different forms.

"You two start this before the sun's up, or did we miss the beginning?" he asked.

"We've been married longer than most people have been alive," Liam said. "There was no beginning."

Maeve didn't look at him.

"Don't encourage him."

"Alright," Gus said. "We're up."

“You’ve got a whole house across the meadow,” Gus said. “And we’re all in here?” Gus asked…no one answered.

The house filled quickly with sound after that.

Movement. Voices. The scrape of chair legs and the thud of boots near the door. Jo tied her thick auburn hair back as she moved through the small kitchen, shifting around Gus without thinking, handing him what he needed before he asked.

"Eggs?" he asked.

"If the hens have done their job."

"They always do."

"They didn't last week."

"That was one time."

She gave him a look.

He grinned.

Liam pushed back from the table and stood.

"You planning on feeding those animals today or just talking about it?"

Liam Callahan didn't wait for an answer. He stepped outside as a swirl of cold blew in before the door swung shut.

Maeve followed a step behind, rising with more care, and pulled her scarf over her head. She threw open the door and called after Liam.

"They've been up five minutes," she said. "Let them breathe, Liam."

"They can breathe after they work," Liam yelled back.

Gus glanced over his mother's shoulder at his father.

"You been up all night thinking about that one?" he yelled out into the morning chill.

Liam snorted.

"Don't need all night. Comes natural."

Maeve shook her head, already moving to go down the steps.

"Move," she said to Gus, not unkindly. "You're in the way."

"I live here," he pointed out.

"Doesn't mean you're useful in that spot."

Jo bit back a smile.

"Jo, get your coat, see you boys in a few for breakfast, Gus."

Gus stepped aside.

* * *

The kitchen in the big house filled in around them.

Not crowded, just lived-in.

Maeve moved through the space like she knew it better than Jo did — which, of course, she did. Her hands were quick and efficient, adjusting things without asking.

"Too much heat," she muttered, shifting the pan Jo had set.

"It's fine," Jo said.

"It's not fine."

"It was going to be."

Maeve gave her a look and patted her cheek.

"You'll get there."

Jo raised a brow and looked down her nose at her shorter mother-in-law.

"I'm already there, Ma."

Maeve snorted a laugh.

"We'll see."

Liam settled himself near the table, watching the room like it was a show he'd seen a hundred times and still enjoyed.

"You're building that north wall today?" he asked Gus.

"Yeah."

"About time."

"It's been time."

"Then why isn't it done?"

Gus glanced at him.

"Because I don't work at your pace."

"You should."

"I'd break something."

"That's because you don't listen."

Gus smiled faintly and chuckled.

"That's definitely the problem."

Jo stepped outside with her basket a short while later. The cold caught her breath for just a second before she settled into it.

The yard stretched out in front of her — small, workable, familiar.

Chickens scratched near the side fence. The goats shifted in their enclosure, already aware of her presence.

Beyond that — trees. And then more land than they could use.

For now.

Gus came up beside her, tugging his gloves on as he looked out over the same stretch.

"You're thinking again," he said.

"I do that."

"Dangerous habit."

"So you've said."

He nodded toward the far edge of the property.

"You planning on expanding out there?"

"Not here," she said.

He glanced at her.

"Not here?"

Jo shook her head.

"Someday," she said, "we'll have something bigger and set apart."

Gus huffed softly.

"Bigger than this?"

"Much."

"With what time?" he asked. "Or money?"

She shifted the basket on her arm.

"We will have both eventually. God provides."

He looked back out at the land, then at her again.

"And what are we putting on this imaginary piece of land?" he asked.

Jo didn't hesitate.

"Room," she said. "For everyone."

Gus let out a quiet laugh.

"Everyone. Everyone who?"

"Family," she clarified.

He nodded slowly, not dismissing it — but not buying it either.

"Alright," he said. "We'll put that on the list."

She didn't laugh. She looked out past the fence instead, past the line where their land ended and the rest of the world began.

Something bigger. Something built. Something solid and strong and theirs.

Behind them, the house stood quiet and steady, smoke rising clean from the chimney. Maeve's voice carried faintly through the walls. Liam answering her without missing a syllable. Marcus already moving along the fence line.

Gus beside her.

Solid and warm.

Jo adjusted the basket and stepped forward into the cold.

"Come on," she said.

Gus followed.

The day waited. The future still somewhere ahead — not yet urgent.

But already there.

CHAPTER 2

The Night It Broke

The house was loud that night.

Not with anything unusual—just the steady rhythm of people living life together, voices crossing over each other, boots thudding, chairs scraping, and the low hum of conversation that never quite stopped.

Liam sat at the head of the table like he always did, one hand wrapped around a chipped mug, the other gesturing as he talked. Marcus leaned forward, arguing something that didn't matter nearly as much as he thought it did.

Gus didn't say much.

He never did.

Jo watched.

She'd found her place there without meaning to—just off to the side of it all, taking in the way things worked. The way Liam carried the room without raising his voice. The way Maeve moved through it, quiet and certain, setting things right before anyone noticed they'd gone wrong.

"You're doing it wrong," Marcus said, half-grinning, pointing at something Gus had fixed earlier that day.

Gus didn't look up. "Still standing, brother."

"For now."

Liam huffed a laugh. "That's most things, son."

He leaned forward, resting his forearms on the table. "You don't build something to never fail. You build it so it holds when it does."

Gus glanced up at that.

Didn't respond.

But Jo saw it settle in his mind.

Maeve stepped behind Jo's chair, setting down a plate, her hand resting briefly on Jo's shoulder. Warm. Steady. Grounding.

"You'll learn," she said quietly.

Jo looked up. "Learn what?"

Maeve smiled, small and knowing. "What matters."

Jo held her gaze a second longer than she meant to.

Across the table, Liam kept talking. Marcus kept arguing. Gus went back to eating like nothing had shifted.

But something had.

Later, the house settled.

The noise faded to something softer, smaller. A door closed. A boot scraped. Someone laughed in the next room and then didn't.

Jo stepped outside for a moment of quiet.

Maeve was already there.

"You don't rest much," Jo said.

Maeve shook her head slightly. "Rest comes later."

Jo leaned against the railing beside her, looking out over the dark line of the trees.

"You make it look easy," she said.

Maeve glanced at her. “It isn’t.”

Jo waited.

Maeve folded her arms loosely, considering her.

“This place doesn’t work because everything goes right,” she said. “It works because when something goes wrong, we don’t let it take everything with it.”

Jo felt that settle somewhere deeper than she expected.

“You’ll hold that line someday,” Maeve added.

Jo blinked. “Me?”

Maeve nodded once.

No hesitation. No doubt.

Inside, Liam’s voice carried faintly through the walls.

Gus answered him this time.

And for a moment—

Everything held.

* * *

It started with a sound that didn't belong.

Marcus heard it first.

He was outside, just beyond the low fence line, checking where the posts had shifted under the last freeze. The cold had driven itself deep into the ground that week, hard enough to crack things that usually held.

The night was quiet.

Too quiet for that kind of sound.

A sharp crack. Wood against force. Not wind. Not settling.

Marcus straightened, straining to listen.

There it was again. Muffled. Wrong in a way he couldn't say, but recognized deep in his gut.

The house lights still burned. Gus and Jo had long since retired to their place, but Maeve kept the lights on late. Said she didn't trust a dark house. Liam had pushed back on it once or twice before he figured out that particular argument was already settled.

Marcus was moving before the thought fully formed.

Not running, but he was moving fast enough to close the distance.

Another sound.

Clearer this time.

A man's voice, but not Liam.

Marcus broke into a run.

The yard stretched out longer than it had any right to. Each step hit harder than the last, breath cutting sharp in his chest, the house growing closer while something deep in him caught up with what he already knew.

The door was open slightly.

A blade of light fell across the snow.

Marcus slowed.

One second. Two.

Long enough for the world to shift beneath him.

Then he pushed through. Fear squeezed his chest.

"Ma?"

He hadn't meant it to come out like that. It wasn't a question, exactly. Just a word thrown into the dark, trying to make the space answer back.

It didn't.

He stepped inside.

The air was wrong. Still warm, but wrong in the way a room gets wrong after something has already happened inside it. The smell hit him then. Not woodsmoke. Not food. The metallic edge of blood.

Marcus held still.

His eyes moved slowly and deliberately across what was there.

And what wasn't.

A chair on its side.

Something broken near the table.

No movement or sound.

* * *

"Da?"

Nothing.

He took another step.

Then another.

The sound of his own boots on the floor felt too loud. Too heavy. Like he was disturbing something that had already come to rest.

He saw Liam first. Not all at once. A shape where it shouldn't be. On the floor, still.

Marcus stopped.

His breath didn't come the way it should. Didn't come at all for a second.

"Da?"

He took a shuddering breath, "No..."

It came out quiet. Not denial. Just a word that couldn't change anything.

He didn't remember crossing the room. Didn't remember dropping to his knees. Just the cold of the floor seeping through his jeans, and the weight of something he couldn't make sense of settling hard in his chest.

"Oh Da—"

He reached out. Stopped. Didn't touch.

Maeve was further back. Near the kitchen. Marcus saw her without turning his head fully, the way you don't look straight at a thing when some part of you already knows what it is but doesn't want to.

It didn't help.

The house held its silence and gave nothing back. No explanation, no reason. Just stillness, deep and absolute.

Marcus pushed himself up too fast. The room tilted. His hand caught the edge of the table, and he steadied, then moved.

Out.

Back into the cold. The air hit him hard, but clean.

He didn't stop. Didn't think about direction.

He just ran.

* * *

Gus saw him coming before he heard anything.

That was what he would remember later. Not the words.

Just the way Marcus moved. His eyes wide, his face just…wrong.

Jo stepped out onto the porch just as Marcus cleared the tree line.

"Marcus—?"

He didn't slow. Didn't answer.

He stopped a few feet short of Gus, breath tearing out of him in ragged pulls.

"Something's wrong," he said.

Gus was already moving. "What happened?"

Marcus shook his head. "I don't— I heard—Hurry…"

That was enough.

"Jo." Just her name, nothing else.

She didn't ask. Didn't hesitate. She turned and moved inside, already reaching for what they may need without being told.

Gus didn't run. He moved fast, controlled.

Marcus fell in beside him, and neither of them spoke.

The house came into view. Door still open. Light still burning inside.

Too still.

Gus slowed.

Marcus didn't. He reached the door first, stopped just short of crossing the threshold, and stayed there. He couldn't go in.

Gus stepped past him.

Inside, the world narrowed. Not visually, not physically, but the way everything else drops away until only what matters remains.

He saw it. All of it. At once.

He didn't react. Didn't speak.

Behind him, Marcus stood in the doorway. Not crossing in, but not leaving either. Just held there, like a man caught between two terrible places with no good ground between them.

Gus closed his eyes and exhaled once. Slow and shaky.

Then he opened them and stepped forward.

He checked Liam first. Then Maeve. The motions were automatic. Practical. Final.

Nothing to be done.

He stood there a moment longer than he should have.

Then turned.

Marcus was still in the doorway. Eyes fixed on nothing.

"Go get Jo," Gus said.

Marcus didn't move.

"Now, Marcus."

That did it.

He turned and left at a run.

Gus stayed.

* * *

He closed the door.

Not all the way. Just enough to hold the space.

By the time Jo came back, the cold had already crept into the edges of everything.

She stopped at the threshold.

Looked at Gus. Then past him.

She didn't cry. Not right away.

She stepped inside and walked the same path Marcus had. Saw it the same way — all at once.

Her hand came up to her mouth. Not to stop anything, but to hold something in place.

Gus didn't touch her. Didn't say a word. He stood there, close enough to feel her presence.

After a moment, she lowered her hand. Looked at Maeve. Then Liam. Then back at Gus.

"This doesn't stay with us," she said in a quiet voice.

Just truth, plain and hard as river stone.

Gus held her gaze, then nodded. Once.

She reached for the phone and called the sheriff.

Outside, the night carried on like it hadn't noticed. The cold settled deeper. The yard stayed still.

Inside, the world had already shifted, and there wasn't a thing in it that could put it back.

CHAPTER 3

After

Morning came whether they were ready for it or not.

It always did..

The light was thin against the snow, pushing through the windows like nothing had changed. Like the world hadn't tilted on its axis in the space of a single night.

Inside, the quiet was different than it used to be.

Not empty, but close enough to feel like it.

Jo hadn't slept. No one had.

The sheriff had come and gone.

She sat at the small table, hands wrapped around a mug she hadn't touched, staring at the middle distance while the fire burned low and steady beside her. The flames burned, indifferent to their suffering.

Gus had been up and moving well before the light.

He hadn't said a word when he moved past her. Just pulled on his coat, stepped outside, and closed the door behind him with a gentleness that didn't match the weight of what the night had taken from them.

Marcus hadn't gone home. He stayed with them at the little house.

He sat near the wall, back flat against it, knees drawn up, eyes fixed on the floorboards like he was trying to hold onto something that kept sliding away.

No one had told him to stay.

No one had told him to go.

The house still smelled like them.

Maeve's cooking. Liam's pipe. Woodsmoke that had worked itself into the beams over years of hard winters and good ones.

Jo noticed every bit of it. Understood the weight of it all.

Filed it away without meaning to, the way grief does, before you know it's doing it.

A knock came mid-morning. Not loud. Not hesitant either.

Gus opened the door.

Two men stood on the porch, hats in hand, boots dusted with snow. Neighbors. Not the close kind, but close enough. The way country people are.

"We heard," one of them said. "We're sorry."

Gus nodded.

That was the whole of it.

They didn't ask questions. They stepped inside, read the room the way men out here learn to read weather, and moved into what needed doing without being pointed at it.

That was how things worked out here.

No one said it. Everybody knew.

Jo stood when they passed her. Not because she had to. Because sitting had become something she couldn't do anymore.

"Thank you," she said.

One of them nodded once.

"Of course."

The day filled with motion after that. Steady and quiet, settling where it needed to.

Wood brought in. Water heated. Liam and Maeve tended to in the way that mattered now, with no ceremony and all the care in the world.

Marcus didn't move at first.

He watched.

Then, slowly, he got to his feet. Stepped in. Took direction without needing it spoken aloud. Held things where they needed holding. Carried what needed carrying.

His hands shook once.

Then they didn't again.

* * *

Gus worked the way he always had.

Focused.

Deliberate.

He didn't speak unless something needed saying. Didn't stop unless something required it. The same rhythm he brought to every build, every repair, every task that needed doing, and wouldn't wait on feelings.

Only this time, there was nothing to fix, and the feelings were heavy.

By afternoon, the house felt different. Not lighter, but more settled. Like the worst of the shock had wrung itself out, leaving something else behind in its place. Something quiet and heavy. Father O'Hara had come to sit with Jo, Gus, and Marcus, bringing his quiet comfort.

They buried them, after the service, but before the light faded in the old St Patrick's cemetery on the hill.

The ground was hard. It took time. No one complained. No one rushed it. Gus refused the offer of equipment to dig the graves. He, Marcus, Jo, and some neighbors dug them by hand. Their heavy breathing created plumes of water vapor in the cold air.

When Father O'Hara rose to speak, quiet fell over those assembled. Jo stood beside Gus. At some point, her hand found his and stayed there. Present.

Marcus stood on the other side of her. Closer than he'd been the day before. Closer than he'd been in a long time.

Liam's voice didn't fill the space the way it always had. Maeve's voice didn't follow it. The silence they left behind was heavier than words.

When it was done, no one lingered. The men who'd come to help nodded once and left the way they'd arrived, quiet and respectful, without asking for a thing in return. The old priest walked with them back to the house before he took his leave.

"Call if you need anything, Gus." He said on his way out.

The big house was colder when they went back inside. It was not because the fire had gone out, but because something was missing from it.

Jo stood in the kitchen for a long moment, her eyes moving over the table, the stove, the small details Maeve had kept in order without ever thinking twice about it. She reached out and adjusted one of them. A cup, sitting slightly off center on the shelf. She set it straight.

Gus leaned against the doorframe, watching her. He didn't want to interrupt.

Marcus stayed near the wall. Not sitting this time.

Jo turned. Looked at both of them, then at the room, then back again.

"We're not doing this halfway," she said, looking at Maeve's apron hanging on its hook.

Her voice was steady. Not raised or emotional. Just clear.

Gus didn't ask what she meant. He knew her and knew what she meant.

"We learn," she went on. "Everything we should've known before." She paused, and the quiet settled between them like cold air through a drafty window. "We don't wait."

Marcus lifted his head and met her eyes. For the first time since that horrible night, something lived in his expression that wasn't just shock. Something sharper.

Gus pushed off the doorframe. "Alright," he said.

It wasn't agreement. Not exactly. It was something closer to commitment.

Jo nodded once.

Outside, the cold settled in as the sun dropped behind the tree line. The land didn't change. The house didn't move. The world kept going, indifferent as it always was.

Inside, they had already begun.

Not all at once. Not loudly. But in the way that mattered.

The line had been crossed. And none of them would be going back to the way things were before.

CHAPTER 4

The First Changes

Marcus didn't go home. Not that first night. Not the second.

By the end of the week, it stopped being something anyone remarked on.

His boots lived by the door. His coat shared a peg with Gus's. Nights, he stretched out on the worn sofa in the front room, one arm thrown over his eyes like he could shut out whatever came for him when the house went quiet.

The tiny house seemed to make room for him.

Jo added a blanket to the sofa. Shifted a chair to open space where there'd been none. Adjusted the rhythm of meals without once mentioning she'd done it.

Marcus noticed. He said nothing.

He just made himself useful in ways that didn't require asking.

Wood was stacked before it ran low. The bucket filled before it emptied. The fence line walked twice when once would've done.

Gus let him.

That was the whole of it. He knew work could heal.

Gus worked even harder after that.

Not longer hours — those had always been long — but with a weight behind it that showed in the set of his shoulders, in the way he came through the door at night with fewer words than he'd left with that morning.

He didn't talk about it. Not to anyone.

Except Jo.

It came out in pieces.

Late, when the fire had burned itself to coals, and Marcus had gone still on the other side of the wall. When the house settled into that soft hollow between exhaustion and sleep.

Gus sat at the edge of the bed, elbows on his knees, hands hanging loose between them.

"I should've been there."

Jo didn't answer right away.

She crossed the room instead, slow and deliberate, and lowered herself beside him without reaching for him at first.

"You weren't. You couldn't have known," she said.

It wasn't comfort. It was truth.

His jaw tightened.

"They didn't— " He stopped. Drew a breath. Started again. "They didn't have anything worth taking."

Jo turned her head slightly, watching him.

"It wasn't about that," she said.

He shook his head once.

"I know."

Knowing it didn't change anything.

She took his hand then. Held it without squeezing. Just present. Just there.

"What if Marcus had been in the house, Jo?"

"He wasn't," Jo answered softly

Gus's shoulders tightened before he pulled it back.

"We're not living like this anymore," she said quietly.

He looked at her.

She held his gaze steady.

"Not with him." A small tilt of her head toward the front room. "Not with us."

She cupped his face in her palm and made him look at her.

"We learn," she said. "Everything we don't know yet."

Gus looked down at their joined hands.

Then back up at her.

He nodded, his eyes glassy and his face creased.

"Okay, we learn. All of it. Together."

This time it carried weight.

This time it had roots.

* * *

The days shifted after that.

Not all at once.

Just enough to notice, if you were paying attention.

Jo started asking questions.

It was what she did, she always had.

But now she followed the answers further.

It was Maeve's old neighbor, Mrs. Donnelly, who started it.

Jo spotted her at the general store, standing near the back counter with a butcher's paper bundle tucked under her arm. The smell gave it away before anything else. Fat. Rendered or not, Jo couldn't tell.

Mrs. Donnelly caught her looking.

"You need something?" she asked.

Jo shook her head. "No." Then, after a moment— "What do you use that for?"

Mrs. Donnelly glanced down at the bundle. "This? Leaf fat, suet."

Jo frowned slightly. "I know what it is. I don't know what you're doing with it."

The older woman studied her.

Then nodded once. "Come by," she said. "I'll show you."

Jo went.

Not that day, but bright and early the following day she headed out for the 1 mile walk to Mrs. Donnelly's place.

The kitchen was warmer than expected. Not from the fire alone, but from use. From something being made.

Mrs. Donnelly didn't explain much at first. She just worked. Cutting the suet down into smaller pieces. Slow. Methodical.

Jo watched. Then stepped closer.

"Why not just use oil?" she asked.

Mrs. Donnelly snorted softly. "Oil runs out. This doesn't."

Jo tilted her head slightly. "That's it?"

"That's enough. The animal fat keeps longer than plant oil too."

They worked in quiet for a while. Fat melting down slow in a heavy pot. The smell was thick, but not unpleasant. Something solid turning into something useful.

Jo leaned in, watching the change.

"You cook with it?" she asked.

"Sometimes. Mostly for other things."

"What things?"

The older woman glanced at her. "You always ask this many questions?"

"Yes."

The corner of Mrs. Donnelly's mouth shifted, just barely.

"Soap," she said. "Candles. Salves, if you know what you're doing."

Jo's attention sharpened. "Salves?"

"Burns. Cuts. Dry skin. Mix it right, it'll hold whatever you put in it."

Jo went still.

Then: "What do you put in it?"

Mrs. Donnelly watched her longer this time. Measuring.

Then she turned and reached for a small jar near the window.

"Depends what you're trying to fix," she said.

She handed it over.

Jo took it carefully, unscrewing the lid just enough to catch the scent. Sharp. Green. Something she didn't recognize.

"What's in this?"

Mrs. Donnelly wiped her hands on a cloth. "Yarrow. Comfrey. Bit of pine resin."

Jo's brow furrowed. "You grow that?"

"Some."

"And the rest?"

"Find it."

Jo nodded slowly, something settling into place.

Not all at once.

But enough.

"Can you teach me?" she asked.

Mrs. Donnelly studied her a moment longer. Then, "If you're willing to listen."

"I am."

* * *

That was how it started.

Not with a plan.

With a question.

At home, the changes showed up quieter.

Gus brought back more than he needed from jobs now. Scrap wood. Extra nails. Things most people would've left behind.

He didn't say why. He just stacked them. Sorted them. Kept them.

Marcus watched. Then started doing the same.

"You planning something?" Marcus asked one afternoon, watching Gus line up boards along the side of the house.

Gus didn't look up.

"Always."

Marcus nodded once.

Jo came in later that evening with her hands smelling faintly of something green and unfamiliar. Gus noticed.

"What's that?" he asked.

She set the basket down on the table.

"Learning," she said.

He glanced inside. Jars. Cloth. Something wrapped in paper.

"You gonna tell me what it is?" he asked.

She smiled slightly.

"Eventually."

He huffed.

"Alright then, be that way."

That night, after the house had gone quiet, Jo stood from the table too quickly. The room tilted. Not sharply. Just enough. The edges of her vision pulled in, narrowing for a moment before snapping back.

She steadied herself against the chair.

Gus looked up immediately and reached out a hand to steady her.

"You alright?"

Jo nodded once.

"Yeah." She exhaled through her nose. "Just stood up too fast."

He watched her a second longer. Then nodded.

"Alright, but sit down, Jo."

She sat back down and waited for the world to settle. It did. She didn't mention it again. At least not that night.

Outside, the cold held. The land stayed the same.

But inside, small things had started to shift. Quietly. Deliberately.

They weren't ready. Not yet.

But they were no longer standing still.

CHAPTER 5

Learning the Shape of Things

Spring came slowly.

Not all at once, not in any way that felt certain. Snow pulled back in patches, then crept in again overnight just to prove it still could. The ground softened where the sun reached it and stayed iron-hard where it didn't.

Everything sat somewhere in between.

Marcus took over the mornings.

No one assigned it to him.

He just started doing it.

Fire first. Then water. Then the quick walk of the fence line before the day settled in around them. By the time Gus came out, most of what needed starting had already been started.

Gus noticed.

He didn't say a word; he merely adjusted.

"You know that loose post on the north side of the field?" Marcus said one morning, not looking up from where he was pulling on his gloves.

Gus nodded.

"I'll get to it."

Marcus shook his head.

"I already did."

Gus looked at him then. Held there a moment.

Marcus met his eyes, steady.

"Alright," Gus said.

That was it.

Jo watched from the doorway, a mug warming both hands.

Not the words.

The space between them.

Something had shifted there. A filling in where things had gone thin.

Her own days moved differently now, too. Less scattered. More deliberate.

She still wrote, early, before the house filled with noise and motion, but the rest of her time stretched into places it hadn't reached before.

Questions didn't stop when she got an answer.

They led somewhere.

* * *

Mrs. Donnelly's kitchen became one of those places that leaves a mark on you.

Jo went twice a week at first.

Then more often.

"Not like that," Mrs. Donnelly said, reaching over to adjust Jo's grip on the knife. "You rush it, you waste half of it."

Jo slowed.

Watched.

Adjusted.

"Like this?"

"Better."

The pot sat low on the stove, heat steady, the contents shifting from solid to something else entirely. Jo leaned in, studying it the way you study a thing you know matters. This wasn't just learning. It was storing, healing, and security.

"How do you know when it's done?" she asked.

Mrs. Donnelly didn't look up.

"You watch it."

"I am watching it."

"Then keep watching."

Jo exhaled quietly and held her tongue.

Later, when the liquid had cleared and the solids had settled, Mrs. Donnelly gave a single nod.

"Now," she said.

Jo moved forward. Careful. Deliberate. She poured too fast the first time, caught herself, and started again. Better.

"Most people don't have the patience for it," Mrs. Donnelly said.

Jo set the jar down, eyes still on it.

"I do."

The older woman glanced at her sidelong.

"Yes," she said. "I can see that."

Then she smiled, "Most of the time."

They moved on to the plants after. Outside, where the ground had just started to give, the earth was still cold and dark beneath the leaf litter.

"This one," Mrs. Donnelly said, crouching down and brushing aside the top layer. "You'll walk past it a hundred times before you see it."

Jo knelt beside her, her knees protesting against the cold ground.

"Yarrow," she said, recognizing it now.

Mrs. Donnelly nodded. "What's it for?"

Jo hesitated. "Bleeding. And inflammation."

"Good. What else?"

"Fever?"

"Sometimes." A pause stretched between them. "What you don't know'll matter more than what you do. Don't guess."

Jo nodded once. "I won't."

* * *

At home, the table changed.

Not dramatically…but enough to be noticed.

Jars lined one edge now. Cloth bundles tucked into corners. A notebook open more often than it was closed.

Jo wrote between tasks — quick lines, short notes, things that wouldn't stay in her head unless she put them somewhere.

Gus stepped around it without comment.

Marcus did the same.

"Looks like you're building a store," Marcus said one evening, nodding toward the jars.

Jo glanced up, smiling.

"Not yet."

Marcus raised an eyebrow.

"Looks like now."

She smiled again.

"It's learning. Like you should be doing with that schoolwork."

Marcus considered that. Then nodded once.

"Alright."

Gus came in later that night, shoulders tight from the day, hands rougher than they'd been a week before. He paused at the table. Looked at the jars. The notes. Then at Jo.

"You planning on using all that?" he asked.

"Eventually."

"For what?"

Jo closed the notebook.

"For whatever comes, I want to be ready."

He held her gaze a moment longer. Then nodded.

"Alright."

They didn't say more. He had faith in her and her plans.

That night, the house settled early. Marcus stretched out on the sofa, one arm over his face, snarted snoring softly, quicker than the night before. Gus sat at the edge of the bed, unlacing his boots slower than usual.

Jo watched him. Waited, knowing he needed to find his words.

He didn't speak right away. When he did, his voice was quiet.

"I keep thinking about it," he said.

She didn't ask what.

"The door," he added. "How it was open."

He went still for a moment.

"I should've noticed something before that."

Jo crossed the room and sat beside him.

"You weren't there to notice Gus," she said again.

He nodded. Didn't argue. Didn't accept it either.

"I don't like not knowing what happened or what to do next," he said.

Jo looked at him.

" We can't do anything about not knowing what happened. We can do something about what we do next. We learn. Together."

Not pushing. Just there.

He let out a slow breath.

"Yeah."

In the quiet that followed, Jo stood and moved toward the table.

She felt it before she understood it. The shift. Subtle. Familiar now in a way it hadn't been the first time. The room tilted — not fully, just enough to catch her off balance. Her vision narrowed slightly, the edges pulling inward like something closing in.

Her hand found the back of the chair.

She didn't say anything. Didn't call attention to it. She just waited.

Gus looked up.

"You alright?"

Jo nodded once. "Yeah." She steadied herself. "Just tired."

He watched her a second longer. Then nodded.

"Then let's get to bed."

She sat down. The feeling passed. Like it hadn't been there at all.

But this time, she noticed it.

Outside, the thaw continued. Slow. Uncertain. The ground shifting beneath everything they thought was solid.

Inside, they were learning how to stand anyway.

CHAPTER 6

What Holds

The first calf came on a gray morning that couldn't decide if it was done being winter.

Marcus heard it before he saw it.

A low, uneven sound from the far side of the neighbor's pasture — wrong enough to pull him off the fence line and across the field without a second thought.

By the time Gus caught up, Marcus was already over the rail.

"Easy," Gus said.

Not to Marcus.

To the animal.

The cow was down. Breathing hard, eyes wide, her flank moving in short, ragged pulls that never found a rhythm.

Marcus hovered a step too close.

"What do we— "

"Back up," Gus said.

Marcus did. Not far. But enough.

Gus moved in slow and steady, the way he always did when something needed handling without making it worse.

"Get the rope," he said.

Marcus didn't ask which one. He ran.

By the time he got back, Jo was there. She must have seen them from the yard, or maybe she'd just followed the sound the same way Marcus had. Either way, she was already crouched beside the fence, watching.

Not panicked. Focused.

"You've done this before?" she asked Gus.

"Once," he said.

"That enough?"

"It'll have to be."

The cow shifted again, a strained, gutted sound tearing loose from her chest.

Jo leaned in slightly, eyes narrowing.

"Something's wrong," she said.

Gus didn't answer. He was already working it out.

Marcus handed him the rope. Gus took it, looping it quick and efficient.

"Hold here," he said, guiding Marcus's hands into place. "Don't pull unless I tell you."

Marcus nodded, his grip tightening.

* * *

Jo moved closer.

Not out of the way.

"What do you need?" she asked.

Gus glanced at her once.

"Stay where I can see you."

She didn't argue. She just shifted enough to be useful.

Time narrowed. Not into panic...into focus.

"Now," Gus said.

Marcus pulled. The cow strained. Gus worked with her — steady, controlled, not forcing more than the moment would give.

Jo watched everything. The movement. The rhythm. The strain. Where things caught. Where they didn't.

"Again," Gus said.

Marcus adjusted. Pulled when told. Held when not.

It took some time. Exactly as long as it needed to, most likely. Hard to tell in moments like this.

Then a shift. Subtle, but there.

Gus leaned in, hands steady. "Almost." Not to them. To himself.

Jo felt it before she understood it. That familiar pull from somewhere deep. The world tilting — not sharply, but enough. Her hearing narrowed, the edges of sound drawing back like the tide going out.

She didn't move. Tried not to let it show.

"Jo."

Gus's voice.

She blinked. Pulled herself back.

"I'm fine," she said.

He didn't believe her. But he didn't push. Not now.

"Now," he said again.

Marcus pulled. The cow gave.

And then it was done.

The calf hit the ground wet and still.

One second — nothing.

Then it moved. A small, sharp breath.

Life.

* * *

Marcus let out a breath he hadn't known he was holding.

"Is that—"

"It's fine," Gus said.

Jo crouched lower, watching the cow shift, turning toward the calf with that slow, instinctive movement that needed no instruction from anyone. She reached out. Stopped herself. Let the moment be what it was.

The world steadied.

Her vision cleared.

Like it always did.

But this time, she didn't wave it off.

They stayed until the calf was up, until the cow settled, until there was nothing left that needed doing.

Walking back, none of them spoke. The air had shifted. Not warmer, but moving, the way it does just before something changes.

Marcus broke the quiet first.

"That wasn't nothing," he said.

Gus made a low sound in his throat. "No. It was certainly something."

Marcus glanced at him, then at Jo. "You just know how to do that?"

Gus lifted one shoulder. "No. I watched, learned along the way."

Marcus nodded, turning it over. Then, "I want to learn it."

Gus looked at him. Really looked at him, the way he did when he was deciding something. "Alright," he said.

Jo watched that pass between them and felt something settle that had been wanting to for a long while.

Back at the house, she set her hands flat on the table and stood still a moment longer than she needed to. The room held. Gus came in behind her and laid his gloves down.

"You weren't fine," he said.

Jo didn't turn right away. "I am now."

"That's not what I said."

She faced him then. Met his eyes. "I don't know what it is. It passes. Comes and goes with no rhyme or reason to it."

Gus studied her, not alarmed, not calm. Somewhere in the narrow space between the two.

"How often?" he asked.

She hesitated, just a fraction. "Just a few times."

Marcus stood in the doorway without moving.

Gus nodded once. "We'll have it looked at."

Jo didn't argue. Didn't agree either. She reached for the notebook, flipped it open, and wrote something down.

"What's that?" Marcus asked.

She didn't look up. "Not forgetting."

He nodded, like that made all the sense in the world.

Outside, the calf found its legs. Unsteady at first, then stronger. Inside, they were doing the same. Not all at once, not without stumbling. But enough to hold.

CHAPTER 7

The Next Season

Spring didn't arrive so much as it settled in.

One day, the ground held. The next, it gave. The snow pulled back from the tree line and didn't come again. The air softened in a way that had staying power.

Work changed with it.

The fence line stretched farther now. Not dramatically, but enough that it took longer to walk, longer to check, longer to fix when something gave way.

Marcus handled most of it.

Not because anyone had told him to. Because he could see it needed doing, and that was reason enough.

"You missed a spot," Gus said one morning, nodding toward a section near the tree line.

Marcus followed his gaze.

Shook his head.

"I didn't."

Gus raised a brow.

Marcus walked him over, crouched, and pressed the post where it had shifted just slightly off center.

"It'll lean," Marcus said. "Not today. But soon."

Gus studied it.

Then nodded once.

"That's a fact."

Jo stood on the porch with her notebook, watching them. Not watching the correction. Watching the way it was received. That part had changed.

Inside, the table had outgrown itself. Jars lined one full edge now. Cloth bundles sat stacked everywhere. A second notebook had appeared without announcement, its pages already half-filled with tighter, more deliberate handwriting than the first.

Jo moved between the work without hesitation. Less guessing. More knowing.

Mrs. Donnelly didn't correct her as often anymore, which Jo had come to understand meant more than any praise the woman might've offered.

"You're not wasting as much," the older woman said, watching her strain the tallow clean.

Jo smiled faintly. "I'll take that as a compliment."

"As you should."

Outside, the plants had come in stronger. They had always been there, most likely. However, Jo was looking for them now. She knew where the yarrow grew thickest along the fence line, where comfrey pushed up near the shaded edge of the property, where the ground stayed damp long enough to support what wouldn't survive anywhere else.

"What's that one?" Marcus asked one afternoon, watching her kneel beside a cluster of green he would've walked right past.

Jo glanced up. "Plantain."

He frowned. "That's not a plant."

"It is."

"What's it do?"

"Draws out infection. Good for bug bites and stings. Splinters."

Marcus considered that, then crouched beside her. "How do you use it?"

She handed him a leaf. "Chew it."

He looked at her. "Seriously?"

"Seriously."

He hesitated. Then did it. Made a face.

Jo didn't laugh. At least not out loud.

"Then what?" he asked.

"Then you use it. Put it right on the scrape."

He nodded slowly and filed it away.

That was how it went now. Not lessons, but accumulation.

* * *

Gus built the extension without making an announcement about it.

A small addition off the side of the house. Better storage. Somewhere to keep what they were slowly accumulating without it pressing in on the limited space they actually lived in. They were avoiding moving to the big house.

Marcus worked alongside him.

Less instruction passing between them now. More understanding.

"You're overthinking it," Gus said one afternoon, watching his brother measure the same board twice.

Marcus didn't look up.

"Or I'm getting it right."

Gus huffed.

"Same thing, some days."

"The saying says measure twice, cut once. So...." Marcus shrugged like his point had been made.

Jo watched them from the doorway, her hands resting against the frame. The rhythm of it. The quiet back-and-forth. Something steady was taking shape where something else had cracked apart.

It was on a morning no different from any other that Gus finally said it.

"You're going to see someone."

Jo didn't look up from the table.

"I am seeing someone. You."

Gus frowned.

"Jo. You know what I mean."

She set her pen down and looked at him.

"It passes."

"I've seen it."

"I am aware. It passes, Gus."

He held her gaze. He wasn't pushing, but he was not letting go of it either.

"Then we check," he said. "Go see the doctor."

Jo considered that.

"Alright, fine," she said finally.

The doctor's office was two towns over. It wasn't too far, but it felt like it was.

Jo went alone, not because Gus hadn't offered, but because she didn't need him to.

The building smelled of antiseptic and copy paper. Too clean. Too quiet. Jo sat with her hands folded in her lap and watched people come and go, all of them looking like they belonged there more than she did.

The doctor was younger than she'd expected.

"You've been having episodes?" he asked.

Jo nodded. "On and off."

"How long?"

She thought about it. "Since winter."

He asked questions. More than she expected. Fewer than she wanted.

"When you stand," he said. "You feel lightheaded?"

"Yes."

"Heart racing?"

"Sometimes."

"Vision narrowing?"

Jo nodded.

He made notes. Listened without interrupting.

"We'll keep an eye on it," he said finally. Not a diagnosis, but not a dismissal either. "We will run a few blood tests today and have you back in six months."

"Anything I should be doing?" Jo asked.

He studied her for a moment. "Pay attention. When it happens. How often. What you're doing when it starts. Write it all down; that information will help us figure this out."

Jo nodded. "I already am."

He didn't seem surprised. "Stay hydrated. Don't push through it if you don't have to. Sit when you feel it coming on. You don't want to fall or faint."

Jo almost smiled at that.

* * *

When she stepped back outside, the air felt different.

Not better.

Just clearer.

At home, Gus looked up when she came through the door. Didn't ask right away.

Jo set her bag down.

"He says we watch it," she said. "He did some bloodwork."

Gus nodded once. "That enough?"

"For now."

He studied her for a few long minutes, then nodded. "We watch it then."

That night, Jo sat longer than usual. Notebook open. Pen moving slower than it should. Her mind was bouncing all over the place.

The phone rang, and she answered.

"Oh, hello, Dr Kent. "

She paused.

Her eyes widened.

"Thank you for calling. Bye now."

Her hand came to rest low on her stomach.

She felt different immediately. Just there, quiet as a held breath.

She didn't write it down yet.

Instead, she closed the notebook and looked across the room. At Gus. At Marcus. At everything they had built in pieces, without ever naming it.

"Gus," she said.

He looked up.

Jo held his gaze, something steady in her expression now. Something certain.

"He said to wait, but he just called about some of my blood tests. "

Gus stopped reading. His face looked worried.

"Okay, tell me what he said. What do we need to do?"

"I think we're going to need more space."

Gus frowned, slightly confused. " What? Why?"

She didn't look away. "Because," she said quietly, "We're having a baby."

The room went still.

Marcus straightened on the sofa. Gus didn't move. Didn't speak.

Then, slowly, he drew in a deep breath.

"Oh," he said, stunned. "Okay."

This time it wasn't a question. It was the beginning of something else entirely.

CHAPTER 8

The First Year

The first summer came in full.

Not hesitant the way spring had been. It settled over the land and stayed, heavy and green and demanding.

Work filled it. Not in long stretches, but in constant ones. There was always something waiting just behind whatever they'd finished.

Jo moved slower now.

She wasn't weak or incapable by any means. Just aware of her balance, the heat, and of how fast a day could slip away from her if she didn't pace herself right.

"You're doing too much," Gus said one morning, watching her haul a basket that didn't need hauling yet.

"I'm doing what needs doing."

"You don't need to do all of it. And certainly not all at once."

Jo set the basket down. Not because he told her to, but she knew when he was right.

"I don't like sitting still," she said.

"Then don't," Gus answered. "But don't fall over doing it."

She almost smiled at that.

Marcus had stopped acting like a guest sometime in those early weeks. There was no hesitation in the way he moved through the house anymore. No pause before stepping into a task, no waiting to be invited. He just did what needed doing, same as the rest of them.

He belonged.

"You're burning through the wood faster," he said one evening, stacking what remained near the door.

Gus glanced over. "We're using more."

Marcus nodded. "Because there's more of us."

Gus didn't answer, just smiled.

Jo watched that exchange from the table, one hand resting absently against her growing stomach. Still small, but not nothing. They had said it once. They hadn't needed to say it again.

The catalog turned up midweek, folded into the stack of mail like it had always belonged there. Jo picked it up without thinking, flipped through the pages the way she always did, quick at first, then slower where something caught her eye. Seeds they already had. Tools they might need. Diagrams she filed away in the back of her mind without even realizing she was doing it.

Then she stopped.

Not because of the words on the page.

Because of the picture.

A house, set far back from the road. So many trees. Wide porch running the full length of it. Weathered, but not gone. Not even close to gone. Smaller cabins scattered around the main lodge.

And behind it, land. More than they had. More than they could use…now. But someday that may not be the case.

* * *

Jo leaned against the counter, thumb resting along the edge of the page.

She didn't call for Gus.

Didn't say a word.

She tore the page out clean, folded it once, and set it beside her notebook.

That was all.

Dinner came the way it always did. Late enough that the day's work had wound down, early enough that the sky still held some color.

Marcus was already halfway through his plate when Jo slid the folded paper across the table.

Gus glanced down at it.

"Bill?" he asked.

"No."

He opened it. Looked. Didn't react right away.

Marcus leaned in from his side, trying to catch a look without being obvious about it.

"What is it?"

Gus turned the paper toward him.

Marcus squinted. "A house?"

Jo shook her head slightly. "Not just a house."

Gus's eyes came back to her.

"It's a lodge," she said. "Big. Multiple cabins." She said it the same way she'd mention the weather. Matter-of-fact. No pressure behind it.

Marcus leaned closer. "How big?"

Jo reached over and tapped the edge of the page. "Enough land for gardens. Animals. More than one family, if it came to that."

The room went quiet for a moment. Not heavy. Just still.

Gus looked back at the page, then out the window, then at Jo.

"Huh," he said.

Marcus glanced between them. "You thinking about it?"

Jo lifted one shoulder. "Someday."

Gus let out a slow breath through his nose. Not dismissing it. Not buying in either.

"That's a lot of work," he said.

"I know."

Marcus sat back, eyes still on the page. "You could do it."

Gus looked at him. "Yep, we could," he said.

Not would. Just could.

Jo didn't push. Didn't explain or try to dress it up into something bigger than it was. She reached for her fork.

"Just something I saw," she said.

The paper stayed on the table a few minutes longer. Then Gus folded it once more and set it near her notebook. Not thrown away. Not tucked out of sight.

Just there.

Outside, the light stretched long into the evening. The air held steady. The land didn't feel quite so small.

Inside, they ate. Talked about ordinary things. What needed fixing, what needed planting, what could wait another week.

But something had shifted. The shift was not in the way they spoke. It was more in the way they looked at the space around them. Not just for what it was, but for what it might become.

Jo cleared the plates later, moving slower now, not fighting it. As she passed the table, her fingers brushed the folded edge of the page.

She didn't open it again.

Some ideas didn't need repeating. They just needed room to sit. To settle in quiet, the way good things often did, until the time came to act on them.

CHAPTER 9

The First Winter

Clare was born on a night the wind and snow didn't let up.

It pressed against the house in long, steady pushes, slipping through gaps that hadn't quite been sealed the way Gus had always meant to fix. The fire worked harder for it. The walls held. Barely, but they held.

Inside, the air stayed warm.

Mrs. Donnelly came when Marcus went for her. Didn't ask questions. Didn't waste time.

"Boil water," she said, stepping through the door and already tying her sleeves back. "Keep it hot."

Marcus moved.

Gus didn't. Not right away.

Jo was in the bedroom, breath drawn tight, one hand braced against the edge of the bed and the other gripping the blanket like it might steady something that had never been the kind of thing you could steady.

She looked up when Gus came in.

Didn't say a word.

He crossed the room and took her hand. Held it the way you hold something you're afraid of losing.

"You're alright," he said.

Not because he knew, but because she needed to hear it.

She nodded once. Tight. Focused.

Time stopped behaving after that. It narrowed, shifted, broke into pieces that didn't connect the way they usually did.

Gus stayed where he was told to stay. Moved when he was told to move. Didn't argue, didn't ask.

In the other room, Marcus worked without being asked, bringing water and wood and whatever was needed before Mrs. Donnelly had to call for it. He didn't cross the doorway. Didn't look in.

But he listened. He couldn't help it.

The wind kept on outside. Steady. The snow piled deeper and deeper. Unbothered by any of it.

Inside, the rhythm built. Rose. Held. Broke. Built again.

At some point, Jo's grip tightened hard enough to grind the bones of Gus's hand together.

He didn't pull away.

"You're doing fine," he said again. "Breath, Jo."

She didn't answer. But she didn't let go either.

Then it changed. The change did not come a little at a time, it came all at once.

A sharp cry. New.

The room went still around it.

Gus didn't breathe. Didn't move. Didn't fully understand what he was hearing until it came again, and Mrs. Donnelly's voice cut through, level as a fence post.

"There we go."

Jo sagged back against the pillows, breath leaving her in a long, ragged release. Her hand slipped from Gus's. She didn't mean to, but she had no strength left to hold with.

Mrs. Donnelly worked with practiced hands, wrapping the baby in quick, sure movements. Then she turned and looked at Gus like he'd gone simple.

"She's fine," she said, not unkindly. "Both of them are."

She stepped forward and placed the bundle into Jo's arms.

Jo looked down. Everything else fell away from her face.

"She's small," she said.

Mrs. Donnelly made a soft sound in her throat. "They usually are."

Jo smiled. Tired and real.

Gus moved closer, slow and careful, like a man afraid of what he might disturb. He looked down at the small face wrapped in cloth. At the tiny hand that shifted once and then went still.

"She's alright?" he asked.

Jo glanced up at him. "She's perfect."

He nodded, taking in her small, round face, the reddish fuzz of her hair.

Marcus stood in the doorway. He didn't come in yet.

"What's her name?" he asked.

Jo didn't hesitate. "Clare."

Marcus nodded once. Like that settled something.

Outside, the wind kept moving. The world stayed exactly as it had been. Cold. Uncertain. Unforgiving of mistakes.

Inside, something had shifted that couldn't be unshifted.

Later, after Mrs. Donnelly had gone and the house had settled into a quieter kind of stillness, Gus sat at the edge of the bed again. Jo leaned back against the pillows, Clare asleep against her chest.

* * *

"You alright?" he asked.

Jo nodded.

"Yeah."

She let a moment pass.

"Just tired."

Gus huffed softly.

"Yeah. I bet. Our girl is always hungry."

Jo smiled at that.

He looked around the room. At the walls. At the smallness of it. At the way everything felt just a little tighter than it had before.

"We're going to need more space," he said.

Jo glanced at him, a faint smile pulling at the corner of her mouth.

"I told you that already."

Gus nodded.

"Yeah." He rubbed the back of his neck. "Looks like you were right."

She didn't say anything to that. She just smiled a sleepy smile.

Clare shifted slightly in her arms. A small sound, then nothing more.

Gus leaned forward, resting his forearms on his knees, looking at both of them.

"We'll figure it out," he said.

Jo watched him. Knew he meant it.

"I know. I am not worried."

Outside, the wind finally started to ease, not gone but less.

Inside, the house held. Tighter now. Fuller.

And for the first time since everything had changed, it felt like something more than just surviving.

It felt like the beginning of something that might last.

CHAPTER 10

What Grows

Clare changed the house.

It wasn't all at once, but it was in the way everything had to shift around her without anyone saying so.

Mornings started earlier. Nights ended later. Sleep came in pieces.

Jo learned the rhythm first. Not because she wanted to. She really had no choice.

Clare woke before the light most days, small sounds that built quickly if they weren't answered. Jo was already awake by then, more often than not. Sitting up slowly. Waiting for the room to stop swaying before she trusted her feet to the floor.

Gus noticed that. Didn't say a word about it. Just started moving sooner.

"I've got her," he said one morning, already crossing the room before Jo had fully pushed herself upright.

Jo paused. Then nodded. "Alright."

He lifted Clare carefully, the way a man holds something he still can't quite believe is his. She settled against his chest without complaint.

"Rest a little more," he added, not looking back. "You go slow when you get up."

Jo watched him a breath longer than she meant to. Then she swung her legs over the side of the bed. Slower. More deliberate. The room held steady. That was becoming less of a question and more of a calculation.

Marcus took over many day to day chores. He'd already been doing much of it. Now there was simply more to do.

"You missed the lower hinge," he said one afternoon, nodding toward the shed door Gus had rehung.

Gus glanced over. "It's holding."

"It'll sag."

Gus studied it a moment. Then reached for the tools.

Marcus didn't smile. He just nodded and strode off to the next task.

* * *

Clare slept through most of it.

Through the hammering and the movement and the quiet disagreements that never quite rose to the level of arguments.

The house felt smaller now. Not because anything had changed within its walls, but because everything outside them had.

Jo shifted her work around the new shape of her days. The table was no longer entirely hers. She wrote in shorter stretches, carved out smaller windows of time, and learned to stop in the middle of a thought and find her way back to it without losing the thread. It wasn't easy. But she managed.

The jars stayed. The notebook stayed open. The questions didn't stop coming. They just fit differently around everything else.

Mrs. Donnelly came by once a week now. Sometimes to help. Sometimes just to look.

"You're doing alright," she said one afternoon, watching Jo move between the stove and the table with Clare tucked against her shoulder.

Jo didn't look up. "I'm doing it. Mostly."

"That's most of it."

Jo adjusted the cloth at Clare's shoulder and checked her without breaking stride. "Show me that again," she said, nodding toward the small jar Mrs. Donnelly had set on the counter.

"Again?"

"Yes."

Mrs. Donnelly snorted softly. "You don't forget much, do you?"

"No."

"Good," the older woman said. "Then you won't have to learn it twice."

Outside, the garden was pushing up stronger than it had the year before. The rows were straighter. The spacing better. Less wasted ground.

The soil hadn't changed. They had.

* * *

Marcus worked the edges while Gus handled the heavier build — posts, extensions, the slow widening of something that had started too small for what it was becoming.

They didn't talk about it.

The space was tight. The way the walls felt closer now than they had before Clare was born.

They just worked.

It came up anyway.

Late one evening, after Clare had settled and the house had gone quiet in that careful way that came with a sleeping baby.

Gus sat at the table, the folded page still tucked near Jo's notebook. He picked it up without thinking. Opened it. Looked at it longer this time.

Jo watched him. Didn't interrupt.

"It's too much," he said finally.

Jo nodded. "I know."

He glanced at her. "You still thinking about it?"

She shifted slightly in her chair. Clare stirred against her. Settled again.

"Yes."

Gus looked back at the page. At the wide porch. The land behind it. The pond, the pines. All the space.

"That's not just a house," he said.

"Oh no," Jo agreed. "It's not. It's a Lodge."

Marcus leaned in the doorway, listening and not pretending otherwise.

"You could fit more than one family there," he said.

Jo nodded. "That's the point."

Gus exhaled slowly. Set the page back down. Not folded this time. Just there.

"We're not there yet," he said.

Jo didn't argue. "I know."

Marcus looked between them. Then at the house. At the walls. At the space they were already pushing against.

"We will be," he said.

Neither of them corrected him.

That night, Jo stood too quickly. The world tilted — harder this time. Not enough to drop her. Enough to cut her breath short. She paused, her hand found the table, waiting for the room to settle the way the doctor had told her to.

"Jo."

Gus was already up.

"I'm fine," she said with a wave of her hand.

He didn't say a word. He didn't need to, she could read his expression.

She waited. The room settled. It took longer than it should have.

She sat back down without being told. Gus watched her — not really alarmed, but not calm either. They had something building quiet and steady between the two of them.

"We're not ignoring that," he said.

Jo nodded once. "No. We aren't."

Across the room, Marcus stayed quiet. But he didn't look away.

Outside, the night held steady. The land unchanged.

Inside, everything was growing. Not evenly. Not easily.

But enough to see it. Enough to know they weren't building something small anymore.

CHAPTER 11

The Years Between

The years didn't stack up all at once. They accumulated quietly, one layered on top of the next until it was hard to say where one ended and the next began.

Clare learned to walk in the space between the table and the door. Three steps, then four, then across the whole room like she'd always known how.

Marcus was there the first time she made the full crossing. Crouched low, hands out, not touching her — just close enough if she needed him.

"Come on, you've got this," he said.

She didn't hesitate or wobble. She just went.

Jo stood back, one hand resting lightly against the wall, watching. Letting it happen. Something caught in her throat she didn't name, and she thought, not for the first time, how fast the days moved when you weren't looking.

"She's going to be trouble," Marcus said, catching Clare when she ran out of steps instead of slowing down.

Jo smiled. "She already is."

Outside, the fence line stretched farther. Another section added, another piece of the world claimed and made theirs. Gus worked it the way he always did — steady and methodical, seeing the finished shape of things long before they were done. Marcus worked beside him now with less instruction and more understanding.

"You're thinking about it again," Marcus said one afternoon, not looking up from the post he was setting.

Gus didn't ask what he meant. "Yeah."

Marcus nodded once.

"That place is still there. I checked."

Gus set the level down.

"Yeah. I checked too."

Marcus drove the post deeper.

"You could do it."

Gus huffed.

"That's not the question."

Marcus glanced over at him.

"No," he said. "I guess it's not."

Inside, the house had outgrown itself — not suddenly, but steadily. Cole came in the spring, quieter than Clare had been and less demanding, but no less present. The space shrank again around them all.

Jo moved through it with a rhythm that had settled deep into her bones. Feedings, work, notes. Rest when she could get it. She still paid attention, still kept track, because the dizziness hadn't gone away. It hadn't worsened either. It simply stayed, a quiet companion she'd learned to read. She knew when to pause now, when to sit before the world made that choice for her.

Gus watched the way he always had — not hovering, but never quite looking away. "You keeping track?" he asked one night, nodding toward the notebook.

Jo didn't look up. "Yes."

That was enough.

* * *

Marcus noticed too.

He didn't ask, but he noticed.

It was late when it finally came up — not planned, not eased into. Just there, the way the hard things always were.

Clare was asleep. Cole had finally settled. Gus was still outside, finishing something that didn't need finishing tonight but wasn't ready to come in yet.

Marcus sat at the kitchen table, turning a nail between his fingers. Not doing anything with it.

Jo looked up from her notebook.

"You're thinking too loud," she said.

Marcus glanced at her. "I'm not saying anything."

"You don't have to."

He set the nail down.

"Couple guys from town enlisted," he said. "Heading out in a few months."

Jo didn't react right away. Just watched him.

"And you're thinking about it."

Marcus exhaled slowly. "Yeah."

Jo closed the notebook and set it aside.

"Why?" she asked.

He shrugged. "Feels like the next thing."

"That's not a reason."

Marcus leaned back in the chair and looked at the ceiling. "I don't want to stay in one place forever."

Jo studied him. "You wouldn't be. There is no rule that says you have to."

He shook his head slightly. "You know what I mean."

She did. A quiet settled between them — not uncomfortable, just honest.

"What are you afraid of?" she asked.

Marcus let out a short breath. "Wasting time."

"That's a real thing," Jo said.

She leaned back, one hand resting against her stomach without thinking about it. "You don't outrun that by leaving."

Marcus frowned.

"You outrun it by choosing what matters," she said, "and staying with it long enough to build something."

He didn't answer. But he didn't look away either.

"And if that's not here," she said, "then you go. But don't go just because it feels like movement."

Marcus sat with that, turning it over the same way he'd been turning that nail.

"You'd tell me if I was making the wrong call," he said.

Jo shook her head. "No. Of course not."

He frowned at that.

"I'd ask you better questions," she said. "Let you figure it out yourself."

That landed.

Marcus nodded once. "Alright."

* * *

Outside, Gus finally came in, the door closing behind him with its solid, familiar sound.

He looked between them, felt the currents of whatever they'd been discussing, and raised an eyebrow but didn't ask.

Jo picked up her notebook again.

Marcus reached for the nail.

The moment passed.

It was a few weeks later when Jo knew. Nothing dramatic announced it. Just a shift, quiet and certain as the turning of a season.

She sat longer at the table that morning, her hand resting low and still against her middle.

Gus noticed.

"You alright?"

Jo looked up and met his eyes.

"We're going to need more space," she said.

Gus exhaled, almost a laugh. "Yeah, we've been over that."

Jo shook her head slowly. "Not like this." She held his gaze. "I'm pregnant again."

The room went quiet.

Marcus looked up from across the table. Gus didn't move.

Then came a slow nod, deliberate and sure.

"Well then," he said. "I guess we do."

No hesitation in it this time. None at all.

Outside, the land stretched the same way it always had. But inside, the decision had already been made. They just hadn't said it out loud yet.

CHAPTER 12

The Next Step

They didn't talk about it all at once, and nobody came right out and said the thing that needed saying.

It showed up in smaller ways first.

Clare running her hip into a chair that hadn't used to be there. Cole wandering from room to room because there wasn't a quiet corner left to settle in. Jo standing still in the middle of the kitchen, trying to remember what she'd come for, then realizing it wasn't memory failing her — it was the walls closing in.

Gus noticed all of it. He didn't say a word. He just started measuring differently, his eyes tracing the room like he was calculating something he hadn't yet put a name to.

"How far out can we push that wall?" Marcus asked one afternoon, eyeing the side of the house like it owed him an answer.

Gus shook his head. "Not enough to matter."

Marcus nodded once. That tracked.

Inside, Jo shifted sideways to let Clare pass, then again to clear the table, then once more when the noise of everyone pressed in from all sides. It wasn't frustration, exactly. It was awareness, the kind that settles before you name it

That night, the catalog page lay open on the table. Not folded. Not tucked away anymore. Gus looked at it longer than he had before.

Marcus leaned in the doorway, watching. Jo didn't touch it. Didn't need to.

"It's still there," Marcus said.

"Too much for right now," Gus said.

Jo met his eyes and didn't argue. "I know."

A quiet settled between them — not disagreement, not hesitation, just the plain weight of truth. Gus exhaled and pushed the page aside, not away, just out of the center of things.

"We're not there yet," he said.

Marcus straightened. "Then what are we doing?"

Gus leaned back, his gaze moving slow across the room — the walls, the table, the space that had already been stretched past what it was ever meant to hold.

"We move."

* * *

Jo didn't react right away.

"Where?" Marcus asked.

Gus looked at him, then at Jo. "The old house," he said.

The words settled over the room like woodsmoke. Familiar. Not exciting, not new, but solid in the way of things that had always been there waiting.

Jo leaned back in her chair, thinking. The old house had been sitting empty for years, maintained but unlived-in. Too much space for one couple, too much quiet in the walls.

"It's bigger," Marcus said.

"Yeah."

"Closer to the road."

Gus nodded. "Still ours."

That mattered more than anything else.

Jo glanced at the catalog page, then back at Gus. "This isn't the end plan," she said.

"No," he agreed. "It's the next step."

Marcus looked between them, then gave a single nod. "Alright."

That was all it took. No celebrating, no wringing of hands over it. They just turned toward the thing and started moving.

The shift happened over weeks. Gus repaired what needed repairing, Marcus cleared what needed clearing, and Jo sorted through what stayed and what got left behind. Clare trailed through all of it like it was an adventure. Cole slept through most of it.

The first night in the old house, everything felt wider. Quieter.

* * *

The space stretched in ways the old one never had.

Room to walk without turning sideways. Room to breathe without bumping into someone else's life.

Jo stood in the middle of the main room, one hand resting low against her stomach, just standing there taking it in.

Gus came up beside her.

"Better," he said.

"For now."

He glanced at her, and she didn't bother pretending she wasn't still turning something over in her mind.

He exhaled softly. "Yeah."

Across the room, Marcus set down a box and looked around the way a man does when he's measuring something that has nothing to do with square footage.

"This works," he said.

Gus nodded. "It does."

Jo didn't argue, because it was true.

Later, after the boxes were stacked and the others had drifted off, Jo rose from her chair a little too fast. The room shifted under her, not sharply, but enough to matter. She caught the edge of the table and held on, waiting it out until the world settled back into place.

Gus watched from across the room and said nothing.

But he didn't look away either.

Outside, the land stayed exactly as it always had. Inside, they had made just enough room to keep going.

CHAPTER 13

The Shape of Home

The house held more than it had before. Not comfortably, but enough.

Clare's voice carried through every room now — not just sounds, but words. Opinions. Questions that didn't quit once they got started.

"Why?"

"Why not?"

"Why can't I?"

Cole followed a step behind her in everything but determination. If Clare ran, he ran. If Clare shouted, he shouted louder, and most days the quiet didn't stand a chance between the two of them.

"Inside voice," Jo said, not looking up from the table.

"I am inside," Clare answered.

Jo paused and looked up slowly. "That's not what I meant."

Something crashed in the next room. Cole's doing, more or less.

"It was him," Clare said immediately.

"It was both of you," Jo replied.

Clare crossed her arms. Cole looked genuinely offended. Gus stepped in before it could tip any further.

"Outside," he said. "Everybody outside."

Neither argued. They ran, the door banging shut behind them.

The noise didn't stop. It just moved.

* * *

Jo exhaled slowly, one hand braced against the table and the other resting low against her stomach. She stayed there a second longer than she needed to, waiting. The room steadied. It always did. She moved again.

Boone slept through most of it. Still small, still quiet in a way that made Jo check on him more often than the others had needed.

Franklin didn't sleep. He hovered in that space between needing help and refusing it. Three years old and certain about everything.

"I can do it," he said, wrestling with a boot that had twisted sideways.

Jo watched him, trying hard not to step in to speed things along.

"Alright," she said. "I know you can do it."

He worked at it, frowned, pulled harder than necessary. Then got it.

"I did it!"

"I saw. Good job!"

He grinned and ran for the door. Jo turned slightly, tracking him with her eyes until he was outside with the others. The house went quiet. Not silent, just less.

Gus came in a few minutes later, brushing dirt from his hands. "They're turning the fence line into a race track," he said.

"Better there than in here."

He glanced at her. At the way she was standing, the way she held herself now. "You sit at all today?"

"Some."

That wasn't an answer. He didn't push it. Not yet.

Marcus's room sat empty most days. Not untouched, just waiting. His things were still there, kept but not packed away. Letters came instead, not often, but enough. Jo read them at the table, once, then again. Gus read them slower and more than once.

Clare asked questions about them. Cole tried to read over her shoulder.

"He says it's hot there," Clare announced one afternoon.

"Different kind of work," Gus said.

"Does he like it?"

Gus paused. "He's learning."

Clare accepted that. Cole didn't.

"When's he coming back?"

"Not yet."

Cole frowned. Didn't like that answer.

* * *

Tantrums came easier on some days than others. Too much noise, too much energy, too many things not bending to the will of small people who believed the world owed them better.

Jo never raised her voice. Never rushed in to smooth it over. She let them feel the full weight of whatever it was, then helped them find their way back to level ground.

"You don't get everything you want," she said once, calm and steady while Clare cried over something that didn't matter and mattered completely at the same time.

Clare sniffed. "That's not fair."

Jo nodded. "No," she said. "It's not."

Clare didn't like that either. But she listened.

Outside, the land had changed — not in shape, but in use. The garden stretched wider, rows straighter, yields better than the season before. Gus had added to the barn, nothing dramatic, just enough. Marcus would have noticed the difference if he'd been around. Jo did and she wrote it all down.

The dizziness came and went, less surprising now, less disruptive, but never fully gone. She'd learned how to manage it — when to pause, when to sit, when to let a moment pass instead of pushing through it like she still had something to prove.

Gus still watched her, quiet and steady from across the room.

"You tell the doctor?" he asked once, leaning against the doorframe.

"He said to keep doing what I'm doing."

Gus didn't like that answer. He wanted an answer, but he didn't argue. Yet.

* * *

The catalog page stayed in the drawer. Not forgotten, not needed. Just waiting.

It was early evening when the truck pulled up.

Clare heard it first and ran for the door. "Someone's here!"

Cole followed, Boone right behind him. Jo didn't move right away. Something in the sound was familiar, tugging at her like a half-remembered song. Gus was already heading outside.

She followed slower, one hand on the door frame as she stepped out.

Marcus stood near the truck. He was older, though not in the ways that showed immediately. It was in the way he held himself, something that hadn't been there before, a weight he'd learned to carry quietly.

Clare hit him first, full speed. He caught her without thinking. Cole crashed into both of them, Boone not far behind, and Marcus laughed, a little surprised, a little out of practice, like a man who'd forgotten what it felt like to be grabbed onto.

"You got bigger," he said.

"So did you," Clare shot back.

Jo stepped down off the porch. Marcus looked up, and something in his expression shifted, the way a man's face changes when he sees something he didn't know he'd been missing.

"Hey," he said.

"Hey."

She didn't rush him. Didn't need to. He crossed the distance instead and pulled her into a quick, careful hug.

"You okay?" he asked quietly.

"We're all good."

He stepped back and looked at her, his eyes dropping briefly to her midsection. "That new?"

Jo laughed. "Not exactly."

Gus came up beside them. Marcus straightened slightly.

"Sir."

Gus shook his head.

"Don't start that."

Marcus smiled. Just a little.

* * *

"I got a few weeks of leave," he said.

Gus nodded. "Alright."

Jo looked between them, reading the space the way she always had. "Then we'll use it."

Marcus nodded once. "Yeah."

Outside, the kids had already pulled him into something loud and chaotic. Inside, the three of them stood in the easy quiet of people who had learned long ago how to be together without filling the air.

Nothing had changed. And everything had.

The years had filled in around them like rings in old wood. Not easy, not quiet, but strong. Deep-rooted in the way that only time and trouble could make a thing.

Still, there were things none of them could see coming. Not yet.

CHAPTER 14

The Night It Took

The day had been dry, though that was nothing unusual. It had settled into that late-summer stretch where the ground held heat longer than it should, and the grass along the fence line turned from green to something brittle without anyone marking the exact moment it changed.

Gus noticed it, of course. He always did.

"Needs cutting back," he said, nodding toward the far edge of the property.

Marcus followed his line of sight. "Tomorrow."

Gus nodded. The word sat there the way it always did.

Jo spent most of the afternoon at the kitchen table, notebook open but her pen not moving much. The younger boys had worn themselves out early. Franklin and Boone were sprawled on the floor with something half-built between them, arguing in low voices that hadn't quite risen to trouble yet.

"Mine."

"No, it's not."

"It is."

"Mama!"

Jo didn't look up. "Figure it out."

They did. Eventually.

Clare and Cole were outside, their voices carrying in through the open window, bright and sharp and alive in a way that filled the space without crowding it. Jo pushed herself up slowly, one hand braced against the table edge, and waited. The room tilted, just slightly, less than it had the week before but still there. She breathed through it and let it pass.

When she stepped outside, the air felt heavier than it should have, thick in a way that pressed against her skin.

Gus was near the fence line, clearing what he could before the light dropped too low. Marcus worked beside him, faster and stronger, the two of them talking in low, easy tones. Jo watched them for a moment, then turned back toward the house.

She didn't see it start. No one did.

It showed up as a line first, thin and low along the far treeline, easy to miss if you weren't looking directly at it.

Then it wasn't.

"Fire!" Clare's voice cut across the yard sharp enough to stop everything else cold.

* * *

The wind shifted, and that was what did it.

What had been small and contained became something else entirely in the space of seconds. The dry grass caught and the flames ran wild.

"Inside!" Gus shouted.

Jo was already moving. Clare and Cole ran toward her, Franklin not far behind, Boone stumbling after them.

"Go!" Jo said, pushing them toward the door.

Smoke rolled low across the yard, the air turning harsh and hot in a way that didn't belong to any ordinary afternoon.

Marcus grabbed the hose and turned it. Nothing came.

"Damn it Gus, no pressure," he said.

Gus swore under his breath. "Buckets. Get water from the troughs."

They moved fast. But it was already too much, too late. The fire didn't behave the way fire should. It didn't slow or hesitate. It jumped — grass to fence, fence to the outer edge of the yard, and then to the house itself.

Jo felt the shift before she saw it. The heat. The sudden change in the air.

"Gus—"

He saw it.

"Out." His voice was quiet, not panicked, but carrying the full weight of a man who understood what was coming.

Marcus dropped the bucket without argument.

They moved the kids first. Clare was crying, loud and raw. Cole shouted something that didn't quite hold together. Franklin clung close, jaw tight, holding himself still the way small boys do when they're terrified and trying not to show it. Boone reacted to everything—the noise, the heat, the fear in every adult face.

* * *

Jo held the door open and counted them out.

One. Two. Three. Four.

All of them. She stepped back.

Gus grabbed her arm. "Move."

They cleared the yard as the first section of roof caught. It didn't explode or collapse. It simply burned — slow enough to watch, fast enough to know there was nothing left to be done about it.

Marcus stood a few feet away, chest heaving, hands empty now. "We should—"

"There's nothing left to get, nothing worth dying for," Gus said.

Marcus didn't argue.

Jo stood with the children pulled close around her, one hand resting against her stomach, the other holding Clare, who had stopped crying and gone quiet.

Cole pressed into her side. Franklin buried his face against her. Boone clutched her sleeve in his small fist.

The fire moved through the house the way it had moved through everything else. Complete. Unstoppable. The walls held for a while — long enough to make it feel like they might not fall. Then they did.

Jo didn't look away. Gus did, just once. Marcus didn't move at all.

By the time it was done, there wasn't much left. The yard was scorched. The fence line gone. The house — gone. Not nothing, but nothing they could use.

The decision had been made for them.

* * *

The night settled around them as though nothing had changed, the silence pressing in from all sides.

Clare shifted against Jo's shoulder. "Where are we going?" she asked.

Jo didn't answer right away. She let the question sit.

Gus stepped closer, and when Jo looked up at him, he held her gaze steady. No waver in it. No doubt hiding behind his eyes. Just that particular stillness he carried when his mind was already made up and his boots were ready to move.

Jo nodded once, slow and sure.

She didn't reach for the notebook in her apron pocket. The answer had always been there, tucked away like a tool you kept sharp even when you hoped you'd never need it. They'd known this moment would come someday. They just hadn't known it would feel quite like this.

Now it had, and they were ready.

CHAPTER 15

What Remains

They didn't sleep that night.

They went back to the small house. The first one.

The one they hadn't planned on ever needing again.

It was tight, but it stood.

The fire burned itself out long before morning, but the heat lingered in the ground, in the air, in the space where the house had stood. By the time anyone came to help, it was already gone.

The smell of it settled into everything.

They kept the children close.

Clare had stopped crying.

Cole kept asking questions until he ran out of answers that satisfied him.

Franklin stayed quiet, thumb in his mouth, eyes too wide for his face.

Boone drifted in and out, too young to fully understand but old enough to know that something had shifted in a way it wouldn't shift back.

The baby pressed low and steady against Jo's ribs. A constant reminder that forward was the only direction left.

Gus kept moving. Not pacing, not restless. Just moving. Checking the perimeter. Taking stock of what was left, what might still matter.

Marcus stayed with him without asking and without needing direction.

"You see how fast it moved?" Marcus said quietly, standing near what had been the fence line.

"Wind turned it," Gus said.

Marcus exhaled. "We couldn't have stopped it."

Gus didn't answer, but he didn't disagree either. That was enough.

Jo sat on the tailgate of the truck with a blanket wrapped around her shoulders and around the children gathered close. Her hand rested against her stomach, still and quiet. She watched the place where the house had stood, not searching for anything. Just taking in what wasn't there anymore.

* * *

Clare leaned into her.

"Is it all gone?" she asked.

Jo looked down at her. "Most of it."

Clare nodded slowly. Cole frowned.

"My things?"

Jo smoothed his hair back. "Yes, but we'll get what we need again."

He didn't like that answer, but he didn't fight it.

The sun came up slow. The light didn't make it better, just clearer. Maybe that was worse.

Gus walked back toward them as it broke over the trees. He stopped a few feet away, looked at Jo, then at the kids.

"We can't stay here," he said.

"I know."

Marcus stepped in beside him. "We could go into town. Find somewhere temporary."

Gus shook his head. "Too many people."

Marcus didn't argue.

Jo looked between them, and the quiet stretched out long and heavy. Clare shifted. Cole kicked at the dirt. Franklin watched everything the way he always did, still and measuring. Boone leaned into Jo and hummed tunelessly. Jo found herself swaying slightly to the sound. Her eyes never leaving Gus's face.

* * *

Marcus looked out over the land, then back at Gus.

"There's the lodge," he said.

The words didn't land hard. They didn't need to. The lodge had been there the whole time, waiting.

Jo didn't move or reach for anything. She just looked at Gus, and he met her eyes. This wasn't a someday anymore.

"It's ready enough," Marcus added. "Structure's sound. We can make it work."

Gus exhaled slowly. Not doubt. Weight.

Jo stood carefully, neither rushing nor hesitating. The ground felt uneven for a second, then steadied beneath her feet. She stepped closer to her husband.

"We don't need perfect," she said. "Never have."

Gus looked at her. "No," he agreed.

She held his gaze. "We need space. We need each other. We need something that will hold." She let that sit a moment. "And we need to move forward."

The words settled between them like stones laid into good ground.

Marcus nodded once. "I can help get you set. I've got time before I have to report back."

Gus glanced at him. "You sure?"

Marcus gave a small shrug. "Where else would I be?"

That answered more than the question.

Clare looked up from where she sat. "Are we going somewhere?"

Jo knelt in front of her. "Yes."

Clare frowned slightly. "Is it better?"

Jo didn't answer right away. She thought about it honestly. "It will be," she said.

Clare considered that, then nodded. That was enough.

Gus took one last look at what remained of the house. Not lingering, not holding on, just acknowledging it the way you acknowledge something that shaped you. Then he turned away.

"Load up what we have," he said.

Marcus moved first. Jo gathered the children. The truck filled quickly, not with things so much as with what mattered.

By the time the sun had fully cleared the tree line, there was nothing left worth staying for. The land sat quiet behind them, scorched and still.

The road stretched ahead. Jo rested her hand against her stomach as the truck rolled forward, and beside her the baby shifted with the movement of it. Life pressing on.

The lodge waited. Not finished. Not perfect.

But standing.

And now, so were they.

CHAPTER 16

The Road That Led There

They didn't say goodbye.

There was nothing left to say it to really. They didn’t have much to take with them, there wasn't much left to take.

The truck moved slow at first, tires crunching over ground that still held the night's heat. Smoke lingered low behind them, thinning as the road pulled them forward and away.

Clare turned once in her seat, then didn't again.

Cole asked questions until the answers stopped changing. Franklin stayed quiet, watching everything the way he always did, taking it in, storing it somewhere deeper than the moment. Boone shifted between wanting to help and not knowing how. The baby pressed steady and insistent beneath Jo's ribs.

Gus drove. Hands firm on the wheel, eyes forward. Marcus rode beside him, not speaking, but thinking plenty.

Jo sat between the children, one arm around Boone, the other resting low against her stomach. She didn't look back. They knew where they were going. They had always known.

The road narrowed as they turned off the main stretch onto packed dirt. A small hobby farm stood at the corner, and an older couple was out working the garden. The man straightened first, one hand on his back. The woman waved. Jo lifted her hand in return.

As they crept along the overgrown lane, branches brushed and scraped the sides of the truck, and the ground shifted soft and uneven beneath the tires. A fallen tree across the road meant they were walking from here.

Clare skipped ahead. "Is this it?"

Jo didn't answer. The heat and the weight of her belly stole her breath on the last mile, and she saved what she had for the walking. The kids ran ahead, whooping and hollering as they approached through the trees.

Then the tree line broke. To open sky. The Lodge stood exactly where it had always been, waiting for them. Not grand, not perfect, but standing.

* * *

Marcus whistled when he stepped into the clearing.

"Still standing," he said.

Gus nodded once and smiled.

The porch stretched wide across the front — weathered boards, railings that would need replacing come spring, a roof that had held mostly but wouldn't forever. The cabins sat scattered in a wide semi-circle around the main lodge, small and rough, but usable.

Jo stepped up carefully and waited for the ground to settle under her feet. It did. She took it all in — not the building itself, but the land. Space filled with possibility, and not a neighbor in sight.

Clare ran up the steps first, Cole right behind her, Boone slower, Franklin last. They spread out without being told, exploring, touching, testing.

"Can we go inside?" Clare called back.

Gus stepped up beside Jo and looked out the same way she did. "Yeah, just be careful," he said.

Marcus was already at the main door, testing the handle. It gave.

The air inside was cooler. Still. Untouched. Dust sat where it had been left for decades, and light cut through broken windows in long, quiet beams.

Clare went ahead, Cole followed, Boone close behind. "Careful," Gus said. They slowed — a little.

Franklin didn't run. He moved slower, eyes scanning, taking it in piece by piece. Jo stepped inside last and paused just over the threshold.

The room was large — larger than anything they'd lived in. Her mind moved without effort, filling the space: tables, people, movement, life. Not just their family, but more than that.

She turned slowly, taking in the structure, the light, the way sound would carry.

Gus watched her. "Well?" he asked.

Jo met his eyes. "It'll do just fine, Gus." That was what mattered.

Marcus moved into the adjoining room and checked the walls, the floors. "Needs work," he said.

Gus huffed. "Yeah. A lot of work." That wasn't a problem.

Outside, the children had already found the edge of the clearing. Their voices carried back toward the house — loud and alive.

Jo stepped back onto the porch and rested her hand against the railing. The wood was rough and worn, but strong enough. Gus joined her.

"You sure?" he asked.

Jo looked out over the land, at the cabins, then back at him. "No," she said.

He nodded. "Me neither."

"But I'm sure enough," she added.

Gus exhaled slowly. "Yeah."

Behind them, Marcus stepped out onto the porch. "We can make this work," he said — not hopeful, not doubtful. Just stating it plainly, the way soldiers do.

Jo nodded. "And we will."

The words settled into the quiet. Not loud, not final, but still true.

“I’ve got a few days,” Marcus said. “Then I head back. We can get you guys settled by then.”

Inside, the children's voices echoed through rooms that hadn't held sound in years. Outside, the land stretched wide and open under a pale sky.

Jo rested a hand against her stomach and felt the baby shift. She'd started turning over names she hadn’t said out loud yet. The family was moving forward.

Gus looked out over it all, then turned toward the door. "Alright," he said.

That was enough. They moved — not because everything was ready or because it would be easy. Because it was time.

And somewhere beyond the treeline, past the quiet stretch of road and everything they couldn't yet see, the world was already beginning to change. They just didn't know it yet.

CHAPTER 17

The First Night

They didn't carry much inside the lodge that first day.

Gus walked it again before the light dropped, moving the way a man moves when he's taking measure of something. Unhurried. He tested doors that didn't sit right, checked windows that would need replacing, pressed his boot to floorboards that held and a few that didn't.

Marcus moved with him, learning the shape of it without asking.

"It'll take time," Marcus said, pushing a door that stuck before giving way.

"Yeah." Gus nodded once.

Time wasn't the problem.

Jo didn't follow them inside. She stood at the edge of the clearing instead, one hand resting low against her stomach, watching the children move through the space like they had always belonged there. Clare had claimed the porch. Cole had found something to question near the steps. Franklin moved slower than the rest, already tracing paths no one else noticed.

Boone dragged a stick twice his size through the dirt like it was a job that needed doing.

They filled the place. Not carefully. Naturally.

* * *

Jo turned when Gus came back down the steps.

"We're not sleeping in there," he said.

She nodded. She'd already known.

"The cabins then?" she asked.

Gus glanced toward them. Small. Weathered. But standing.

"Closest one," he said. "We make that tight first."

Marcus nodded. "I'll get it cleared."

They moved without discussion.

When they pushed the door open, the cabin breathed out dust and old wood. Not unpleasant. Just the smell of a place that had been waiting. Marcus shoved the door wide and let the air move through while Gus walked the perimeter, checking the frame, the roofline, the corners, pressing his palm flat against the timber like he was reading its pulse.

"Good bones," he said. That was enough.

They worked until the light began to thin. Sweeping, clearing, hauling out what didn't belong. Jo moved slower than the rest, more deliberate, the floorboards as she decided where things would go and where they wouldn't. Clare tried to help and mostly got underfoot. Cole asked questions about everything, why this cabin and not that one, why they couldn't just sleep in the big house. Gus answered him once.

"Because this one will hold tonight."

That settled it.

Franklin found a broken hinge and turned it over in his hands like a man solving a puzzle. Boone carried what he could, then what he probably shouldn't have, then went back for more.

By the time the sun dropped behind the treeline, the cabin wasn't finished. But it was ready.

* * *

Gus lit the fire himself, keeping it small and controlled. The warmth came quick in the tighter space, held better than it ever would have in the lodge.

Jo settled the blankets and arranged the children where they fit. Clare near the wall, Cole beside her, Franklin just off to the side where he could watch the door, Boone tucked wherever there was room. Jo lowered herself down last, slow and careful. The room tilted for a second. She waited, and it steadied.

Across the room, Gus watched her. He didn't say anything.

Marcus leaned back against the wall near the door, not sleeping yet.

"I'll head out in a couple days," he said.

Gus nodded. "We'll be set by then."

Marcus looked around the room, taking in the walls, the space already filling with breath and body heat. "Yeah," he said.

Outside, the woods settled into themselves, alive in the way winter woods are alive, full of quiet sounds that weren't silence at all. The fire cracked softly. The air shifted as the heat took hold.

Clare yawned. Cole didn't. Franklin watched the flame like it was telling him something he needed to remember. Boone was already half-asleep.

Jo let her head rest back against the wall. For the first time since the fire, they were inside something that held.

It wasn't much. But it was enough.

* * *

A sound broke it. Small and quick, then again.

Clare sat up. "What was that?"

Cole froze. Franklin didn't move. Boone blinked awake, and Marcus tilted his head slightly, listening.

There. A scratch. A shuffle. Then something darted along the far wall.

Clare gasped. Cole scrambled backward. "Something's in here!"

Boone pushed himself up, eyes wide. "Where?"

Franklin leaned forward, curious rather than alarmed. A small shape slipped along the base of the wall, quick and low, then vanished behind a loose board.

"Mouse," Marcus said.

"Too big for a mouse," Cole said immediately.

Clare pulled the blanket up. "That's disgusting."

Boone squinted toward the wall. "That was cool."

Franklin stood slowly, stepping closer.

"Don't touch it," Jo said.

"I'm not," he answered. But he kept watching.

Gus waited a moment, then crossed the room and nudged the loose board back into place with his boot. "Lives here," he said simply.

Clare made a face. "Not anymore it doesn't," Cole said.

Gus glanced at him. "It was here first."

That settled that. Mostly. Clare still looked unconvinced, Cole looked like he was building an argument, Franklin looked like he wanted to see it again, and Boone grinned at all of them.

Jo exhaled softly. "Everybody lay down."

They did…eventually. The room settled around them, not perfectly quiet, but held.

* * *

Gus sat a while longer after the kids drifted off, watching the fire burn down to coals, listening to the quiet settle around him like something living.

Marcus shifted near the door.

"You good?" he asked.

"Yeah." Gus nodded once. "This'll work."

Marcus took his time answering.

"Yeah," he said finally. "I know it will."

Across the room, Jo's breathing had evened out, one hand resting low and still. Gus watched her a moment, then let his gaze move to the children, to his brother, and then to the walls around them — rough and unfinished, but standing.

Outside, the trees kept their silence.

Inside, the fire burned low and the room held its warmth, and for the first time since everything had been stripped away, they had something again. Unfinished. Uncertain. But theirs.

It would keep.

For now, For now—and for as long as they made it.

The End

Continue the journey with the Callahan family:

The First Stranger - and Early Years Novella

JOIN THE CALLAHAN COMMUNITY

Start reading now: Http://kellyschweigerbooks.com

Get exclusive content, early releases, and behind-the-scenes access to the world of the Callahans.

Download a free bonus content when you sign up for the newsletter! Be the first to know when new books release—and what happens next. Follow me on Facebook, TikTok, or Instagram.

A QUICK FAVOR

If you enjoyed this book, leaving a short review makes a huge difference.

It helps other readers discover the series—and allows me to keep writing more stories like this one.

Thank you for being part of this journey.

About The Author

Kelly Schweiger writes post-apocalyptic fiction centered on family, resilience, and survival in a world forever changed.

Her stories focus on ordinary people facing extraordinary challenges—building, protecting, and enduring together.

When she's not writing, she's spending time with her husband, children or grandchildren.

www.ingramcontent.com/pod-product-compliance
Lightning Source LLC
LaVergne TN
LVHW090530110826
845146LV00003B/1046

* 9 7 9 8 9 9 9 0 9 9 8 8 4 *